THE TREE HOUSE KIDS

The Richest Kid in the World

Carol Gorman

Illustrated by Rudy Nappi

CONCORDIA®

Publishing House
St. Louis

Copyright © 1993 Carol Gorman

Published by Concordia Publishing House
3558 S. Jefferson Avenue, St. Louis, MO 63118-3968
Manufactured in the United States of America

Library of Congress Cataloging-in-Publication Data
Gorman, Carol.
    The richest kid in the world / Carol Gorman : illustrated by Rudy
Nappi.
    (The Tree House Kids : #3)
    Summary: Ben asks God to bless him and his friend Sam with riches,
but a visit to two different homes brings him surprising revelations about
who is really rich.
    ISBN 0-570-04728-5
    [1. Money—Fiction. 2. Wealth—Fiction. 3. Christian life—fiction.] I.
Nappi, Rudy, ill. II. Title. III. Series: Gorman, Carol. Tree House Kids
series : #3.
PZ7.G6693R1   1993
[Fic]—dc20   92-24935

---

1 2 3 4 5 6 7 8 9 10   02 01 00 99 98 97 96 95 94 93

For my editor and friend,
Ruth Geisler

Series

The Biggest Bully in Brookdale
It's Not Fair
The Richest Kid in the World
Nobody's Friend

Contents

Patrick's Birthday Party

"*But you said we could go!*" said Ben Brophy, looking back and forth between his mom and dad. "You *promised!*"

Ben's mother sighed and stared into her coffee cup on the kitchen table.

"Ben, I'm sorry," his dad said. He leaned over his cereal bowl and gently squeezed Ben's arm. "The trip just isn't going to work out next weekend. I didn't realize how expensive the dentist's bill was going to be."

Grady, Ben's four-year-old brother, stood next to Ben, his hand on Ben's shoulder. Usually Grady wanted what Ben wanted, and today was no different. His lower lip stuck out, and he sniffled back tears.

"I want to go to Treat Adventures," he said.

"*Great* Adventures," Ben said, rolling his eyes. "Get the name right, for pete's sake."

"Boys," Mrs. Brophy said to Ben and Grady, "after we pay the dentist, we won't have the extra money this month. I know how much you looked forward to going to Great Adventures, but theme parks like that are expensive."

"And then we'd have to pay for two nights in a motel," his dad said. "Not to mention meals for three days."

"We're trying to pay off our bills, honey," his mother said.

"Great Adventures has a new ride," Ben said. "A triple loop-de-loop in the dark."

"Yeah," Grady said. "A triple loop-de-loop!"

His mother's face turned a slight greenish color, but his father smiled.

"We'll go, guys," his dad said. "I promise you that. We'll go to Great Adventures in a couple of months, and you can ride on all the roller coasters you want."

"Just don't make yourself sick like last time," his mother said. "Grady isn't old enough for roller coasters yet, thank goodness."

8

"I am too," Grady said.

"Dumb dentist," Ben mumbled.

"Dumb dentist," Grady repeated.

"No, it's not fair to blame Dr. Clover," said Mrs. Brophy. "It's nobody's fault. Your dad needed the dental work done—he was in a lot of pain."

Ben set his mouth in a tight little line. "I wish we had lots of money," he said, "like Patrick Doyle. He has *everything!*"

"Aren't you going to Patrick's birthday party soon?" his dad said. "When is that?"

"This afternoon," Ben said.

"That's good," his mother said. "Why don't you think about that and try to forget about Great Adventures? Before too long, we'll have a little extra money and we'll go, just as we promised."

Ben rolled his eyes and sighed. "Okay." He didn't have much choice.

"Can you believe it?" Tess Munro said, stepping through Ben's front door. "We're finally going to Patrick Doyle's birthday party! We'll get to see his *mansion!*"

She grinned and flopped down on one

end of the couch in Ben Brophy's living room. She was dressed in her best jeans and a striped blouse. A canvas bag sat in her lap. "Don't forget your swimsuit," she said. "Remember, Patrick said we get to swim in his *pool!*"

"I wouldn't forget that," Ben said. He grinned.

Ben had spent the morning, after his conversation with his parents, concentrating on Patrick's birthday party. He didn't want to think about what he'd be missing on the trip to Great Adventures.

It was now nearly two o'clock, and Ben was feeling excited about Patrick's birthday party.

"I can't believe he invited the *whole, entire* third-grade class!" Tess said.

"Yeah," Ben said.

"So, are you ready?" Tess said.

"Yup," Ben said. "I just have to tell Mom I'm going."

Ben walked into the kitchen and stopped at the top of the stairs leading down to the basement.

"Mo-ooom!" he yelled. "I'm leaving now!"

10

Ben's mother hurried up the steps. "Okay," she said, smiling. "Have a good time, you two. Are you *sure* you weren't supposed to get birthday presents for Patrick?"

"I showed you the invitation," Ben said. "It said, 'No Presents, Please.' "

"Besides," Tess said, "Patrick has *everything* already! His family's rich!"

"Okay," Mrs. Brophy said. "I guess if they requested no presents—" She handed Ben a cloth beach bag. "Here's your suit."

"Thanks," Ben said. "We'll walk home when the party's over at five o'clock."

"Okay," his mother said. "Have a good time."

"Don't worry about that!" Tess said. "This is going to be *excellent!*"

Ben and Tess walked out the front door and down the sidewalk.

"I can't wait to see the inside of Patrick's house," Ben said.

"I heard the party's going to be on the lawn," Tess said.

"Oh," Ben said. "Have you ever been inside his house?"

"Are you kidding?" Tess said. "Patrick

11

lives in the biggest house in town, for pete's sake. Don't you think I would've *told* you if I'd ever been inside?"

"Yeah, I guess you would have," Ben said. The kids turned right at the corner. "Remember when we stopped to trick-or-treat there last year?"

"Yeah," Tess said. "We only got to step inside the front door. But it was awesome. The ceilings were so high!"

"Remember what their Halloween treats were?" Ben said.

"Those jumbo-sized candy bars," Tess said. "They cost a lot of money. I only get them on my birthday because my mom says they rot your teeth."

"Yeah," Ben said. His eyes glazed over as he walked and thought about Patrick. His parents had so much money they could pay the dentist after the candy bars rotted your teeth and *still* have lots of money to go to Great Adventures.

"Wouldn't you love to be rich?" Ben said.

"I sure would," Tess said. "Think of all the great stuff you could have."

"Patrick has the most stuff of any kid I know," Ben said.

Tess's eyes lit up. "Like what?" she asked.

"Well, the swimming pool, for one," Ben said.

"What else?" said Tess.

"I heard he has his own computer," Ben said. "And his own TV and telephone—he has his own *telephone number*."

"You're kidding!" Tess said.

"Uh-uh," Ben said. "And a housekeeper cleans his room for him."

"Wow," Tess said. "I wish my family had a housekeeper."

"He says he has to pick up his stuff, but Hildy cleans," Ben said.

"Gee," Tess said, "if I had a housekeeper, I bet I wouldn't have to wash the dishes after supper. Ashley and I trade off washing every other night." She rolled her eyes. "That is, we're *supposed* to. But whenever she has a lot of homework, *I* have to wash them— even if it isn't my turn."

"Yeah," Ben said. "I have to empty the wastebaskets and take the trash and the recycling stuff to the curb every week."

"And I have to clean my room every week," Tess said.

"So do I," said Ben. "And I have to help rake and shovel snow and pull weeds in the garden."

"I bet Patrick doesn't have to do all that stuff," Tess said.

"I bet not either," Ben said. "Rich kids have it made."

"You can say that again," Tess said.

"I can see Patrick's house from here," Ben said, pointing over the trees. "See? You can see his roof just over the trees in the park."

Tess looked where Ben was pointing. "Yeah," she said. "Patrick's mansion."

Ben and Tess walked along in silence for the next two blocks. Then they rounded a corner, and the Doyle mansion came into view.

The huge, red-brick house stood back from the street on a gently sloping hill. Five massive white columns stood at the front of the house, reaching as high as the roof over the third floor. A balcony ran along the second floor. Baskets of red and white flowers grew in pots hung over the balcony and in containers sitting on the huge front porch.

"Boy," Ben said. "Patrick's house is as big as a hotel!"

"The party must be in the back," Tess said.

Several cars pulled up in front of the house. Kids from their class began piling out and running up the sloped lawn.

"Look, there's Kara and Nikki," Tess said. "And Rich and Sam!" She turned to Ben. "Come on, let's go!"

Ben and Tess caught up with their four classmates and trudged up the slope to Patrick's house. All of the kids were dressed in their best casual clothes, shorts and crisply ironed shirts. Even Sam Flagg, who usually wore worn and patched jeans bought secondhand from the Salvation Army store, looked specially dressed.

"Look at the sign!" Ben said. He pointed to a banner taped along the railing of the front of the porch. It was yellow with red letters.

WELCOME TO PATRICK'S
BIRTHDAY PARTY!
THE FUN IS IN THE BACKYARD!

15

"Come on," Ben said.

The kids hurried around the side of the big house, and the backyard came into view. They stopped short and stared.

"*Wow!*" Tess said.

"*Double wow!*" Ben said.

The large backyard was decorated in red and yellow. There were red and yellow streamers fluttering from the trees. Red and yellow helium balloons were tied to the patio furniture. Red and yellow beach balls floated in the swimming pool.

A clown, dressed in a red coat and yellow trousers and surrounded by a small group of kids, juggled four yellow balls on the patio. Six kids played badminton at the net set up under the trees. And a game of croquet was going on near the other side of the house.

"Hi, Ben, Tess," called out a voice near the back door.

The kids turned to see Patrick walking toward them. He had a big smile on his face. Patrick was a good-looking kid with light brown hair, which was nearly always neatly combed, and big brown eyes. He was dressed in red shorts and a polo shirt.

"Hi!" Ben and Tess said.

"Patrick, this is *incredible!*" Tess said.

Patrick shrugged. "Thanks," he said, still smiling. "I hope everybody has a good time."

"Are you kidding?" Ben said. "Of *course* we'll have a good time!"

"This is better than a carnival!" Tess said.

A smiling woman wearing an apron and holding a silver tray approached. "Would you like some cookies?" she said to Ben and Tess. "There are four different kinds."

"Thanks," Ben said and picked up a chocolate chip cookie.

"I'm too excited to eat," Tess said.

"*That's* never happened before," Ben said.

Tess stuck out her tongue at Ben.

The woman laughed. Then she turned to Patrick. "Patrick, be sure to greet *all* of your guests." She nodded to Ben and Tess and moved on.

"Is that your mom?" Ben asked Patrick.

"No," Patrick said. "That's Hildy. She's our housekeeper, but she's like one of the family."

"Are your mom and dad inside?" Tess asked.

"No, they're both in Europe," Patrick said. "They'll call tonight, though, I think, to say happy birthday."

"In *Europe!*" Tess said. "How exciting!"

"Well, see you later," Patrick said. "We're going to have a magician and games after awhile. Then we'll swim." He moved off then to talk to some other kids.

"A *magician?*" Tess said, her eyes big.

"A clown *and* a magician?" Ben said. He shook his head. "This is *great*—like something you'd see in a movie!"

"I know," Tess said.

Ben stood on the patio and looked around at the colorful splendor that was in Patrick's very own backyard. Ben felt a funny feeling that wasn't familiar to him. He wished he could take Patrick's place, live in Patrick's shoes, and have all the things Patrick had.

Ben was very, very envious.

Ben turned and looked at Patrick. The boy was talking with a group of kids near the pool. He was laughing and looking very happy.

Why shouldn't he look happy? Ben

thought. Patrick is living a dream, the way every kid in the world wishes he could live. Patrick must be one of the richest kids in the world, Ben thought. He has *everything!*

Prayers for Riches

"And then we swam in Patrick's pool, and then we played tag in the yard," Ben said. "And then—"

"And then we had hamburgers grilled on the patio and the best potato salad I've ever had!" said Tess. "I usually don't like potato salad."

"Hildy, Patrick's housekeeper, and Sarah, their cook, made all the food," Ben said.

"Gee," Roger Quinn said, his eyes wide behind his big glasses, "I wish the second-grade class had been invited."

"Maybe sometime the three of us can go over to Patrick's house and play," said Ben.

"That'd be awesome," said Roger.

The three kids were sitting cross-legged

in the tree house overlooking Mrs. Pilkington's yard. Not long ago, they had formed a club, The Tree House Kids, to figure out what to do about a kid at school who'd been picking on them. After their problem with Brad Garth had been taken care of, the three decided to continue their club meetings.

Ben, Tess, and Roger were the best of friends.

"Patrick is so lucky!" Ben said. "He has so much neat stuff!"

"Yeah," Roger said. "I bet his parents never argue about anything."

"What do you mean?" Ben said.

"Well," Roger said, "it seems like whenever my mom and dad get mad at each other, it's usually about money. I mean, I'm sure they love each other and all that stuff, but they sure can get mad and yell a lot. I hate it."

"Yeah," Tess said. "My mom worries about money too. Sometimes she wonders if we'll have enough to pay our bills."

"Mine too," Ben said, thinking about his family's canceled trip to Great Adventures. "I'm just glad I'm not Sam Flagg. His family's *really* poor."

"Yeah," Tess said. "I feel sorry for him. His clothes are pretty crummy, and his pants are either too big or too small."

"I think I know who he is," Roger said. "Dark hair, and he's kind of tall and skinny?"

"Yeah," said Ben. "He's got three brothers and two sisters. And they all live in that little house on Green Street. He told me he shares a room with all of his brothers!"

"*Four* kids in one bedroom?" Tess said. "Yuck. I thought sharing a room with Ashley was bad!" She thought a minute. "Well, maybe sharing a room with Ashley is *worse* than four kids in a bedroom!"

Ben laughed. "Ashley's not so bad," he said.

"If you like teenagers who hog all the space," Tess said, rolling her eyes.

"Sam asked me to come over after school tomorrow," Ben said.

"Are you going?" Roger said.

"Sure," Ben said. "He's a nice guy."

"Yeah, I like him too," Tess said.

"I hear people talking up there!" a voice called out from below.

Roger stood up and looked over the side

wall of the tree house. "Hi, Mrs. Pilkington!" he said. "Want to come up? The Tree House Kids are having a meeting."

"Is your meeting open to nonmembers?" Mrs. P. asked, a smile in her voice.

"Sure," Roger said. "We'll let *you* up here anytime."

"Great," Mrs. P. said. "Then I'd like to join you. Just let me take the rest of my laundry off the line."

Roger sat back down. "Mrs. P.'s coming up," he said.

"Mrs. P. would make an awesome grandmother," Tess said. "She's so—so—I don't know, she's *fun!* She climbs trees—"

"She skydives," added Ben.

"She takes aerobics classes," Tess said.

"I've been thinking about Mrs. P.," said Roger. "I think we should make her an honorary member of The Tree House Kids. After all, we're using her tree house."

"Yeah," Tess said.

"Good idea," Ben said.

Mrs. P.'s gray head popped into view a few minutes later, and she hauled herself up off the garage roof and into the tree

24

house. She was wearing jeans and a blue T-shirt.

"Hi, guys," she said and plopped down on the floor with the others, forming a small circle. "What's new with The Tree House Kids?"

"We've decided to make you an honorary member of our club," Roger said.

Mrs. P. smiled broadly. "How nice!" she said, clapping her hands together. "I'm honored."

"We should have a ceremony," Tess said.

"Yeah," Ben said. "How about Saturday after we get it planned." Maybe he wouldn't be riding the loop-de-loop in the dark, Ben thought, but at least he'd have *something* fun to do on the weekend.

"Good," Mrs. P. said. "I'll look forward to it." She looked around the circle. "I didn't see you kids here yesterday."

"Tess and I went to the biggest, best birthday party we've ever been to!" said Ben.

"That sounds like fun," Mrs. P. said. "What made it so special?"

"Patrick Doyle is rich, rich, rich!" said Tess.

"Doyle?" said Mrs. P., thoughtfully.

"Does he live in the big brick house? With the white pillars in front?"

"Yeah," Ben said. "We got to swim in their pool. And there was a magician there and a clown and everything!"

"Oh, that does sound exciting," said Mrs. Pilkington.

"Mrs. P.," Ben said. "I've been thinking. Remember when we prayed about Brad Garth when he was beating up everybody in sight?"

"Yes," said Mrs. P.

"And everything turned out okay," Ben said. Mrs. P. nodded. "Well, do you think it'd be okay to pray and ask God to make us rich?"

Mrs. Pilkington smiled. "I think it's okay to ask for anything that you want or need, as long as it won't hurt anyone."

"Really?" said Ben.

"Sure," said Mrs. P. "God wants good things to happen for you. But, you know what? I think you're already rich."

"*Me?*" said Ben.

"And you, Tess. And you, Roger," said Mrs. Pilkington.

"My mother would laugh if she heard you

say that, Mrs. P.," Tess said. "We really don't have much money."

"Neither do we," said Roger.

"We don't either," said Ben.

"I don't mean rich in that way," said Mrs. P.

Tess rolled her eyes. "Oh, you mean, we're lucky that we're not *starving* and we have a place to *live* and all *that* stuff."

Mrs. P. laughed. "Well, that's very true. We've all been blessed with those things. We also have good health, and that's very important."

"Yeah, I guess," Ben said. "But Patrick has everything in the world he could possibly want! He even has his own horse! He keeps it at a stable on the edge of town."

"That would be fun, all right," said Mrs. P. "I like to go horseback riding too."

"Me too," said Ben.

"Maybe he'll take you, Ben!" said Roger.

"I hope so," Ben said.

"But what I'm getting at," said Mrs. P., "is that you all have families who love you. *People*—friends and family—make up the most important riches we can ever have."

"Yeah, yeah," said Tess, waving her hand

impatiently. "So it's okay to ask God for money and stuff?"

"Yes, Tess," said Mrs. P., smiling. "It's okay. But I think before asking for more money and stuff, you should think about all that God has given you already and sincerely thank Him for those magnificent gifts."

"Yeah, okay," said Tess and shrugged.

"I want to be a millionaire!" said Ben.

"Or a billionaire!" said Roger.

"The richest kid in the world!" said Tess.

Patrick's Stuff

That night Ben dreamed he was the richest kid in the world. He built a huge, beautiful mansion for his family with three swimming pools, a tennis court, and a riding stable for horses. He bought his dad three shiny sports cars (red, blue, and yellow) and his mom a fancy computer to keep all the household records.

Then he hired a maid to clean constantly (mostly in his room), a cook (whose specialties were pizza and tacos), a driver who would take him anywhere he wanted to go at any moment he wished, and a gardener to plant lots of flowers and take care of the huge lawn. And he took his family to Great Adventures one weekend every month to ride the roller coasters. Even his mom. And nobody got sick.

Now, if only I didn't have to go to school, Ben thought.

Then he woke up.

He turned over and looked at the clock on the table next to his bed. His alarm would go off in 10 minutes, and he'd have to get up and go to school.

Ben sank back in bed and put his hands behind his head.

If only it hadn't been a dream! How wonderful it would be to have everything you wanted, like Patrick Doyle. Ben had asked God last night to make him rich. Maybe if he prayed hard enough, it would happen for him too.

When his alarm rang, he climbed out of bed and started getting ready for school. He was going to Sam's house after school, so he decided to put on an older pair of jeans and a shirt that had faded in the wash. Poor Sam didn't have nice clothes, and there was no sense in making him feel bad.

Ben met Tess on the sidewalk outside and they picked up Roger on their walk to school. They arrived about 10 minutes before the first bell, so they headed onto the playground.

"Let's get in line for tetherball," said Ben.

"I'll get there first!" Tess said and took off running for the closest tetherball pole.

There were already six kids in line, and Patrick Doyle was at the end. He turned around and waved at Ben and Tess. "Patrick," Ben said, getting into line behind Patrick, "that was a *great* birthday party you had!"

"Yeah," Tess said, "that was the *best* party I've ever been to!"

Patrick grinned. "Thanks," he said. "I had fun too."

"Really?" Tess said. "And you didn't even get any *presents!*"

Patrick shrugged. "I didn't mind," he said. "It was neat having the whole class at my house."

"Hey, this is Roger Quinn," Tess said, turning to Roger. "He's only in second grade, but he's our friend anyway. Besides, he's really smart."

"Hi," Patrick said.

"Hi," Roger said, a little shyly.

"Hey," Patrick said, turning to Ben, "do you guys want to come over after school? I got some really great presents I want to show you."

"*Wow, really?*" Tess said. She looked at Roger. "Can Roger come too?"

Roger stood up straight and tall, hoping that made him look older, and smiled at Patrick.

Patrick grinned. "Sure," he said.

"Great!" Ben said. "We'll meet you after school!"

The four kids grinned at one another, and Ben felt happy.

Well, he thought, while I'm waiting for God to make me rich, I'll just have fun at Patrick's house!

It wasn't until 10:30 that morning that Ben remembered he was supposed to go home with Sam Flagg today.

He remembered it when the class was playing kickball in gym. Sam was playing second base, and when Ben slid into base, Sam said, "Good going, Ben," even though he was on the other team. Then he said, "Want to get up a kickball game with my brothers and sisters after school?"

Ben opened his mouth to say he was going to Patrick's house today, and that's when he remembered he'd told Sam that he'd go over to his house.

What would he do now? He'd promised Sam first, so he really should go there. But he'd disappoint Tess and Roger if he didn't go to Patrick's.

Then he felt guilty. The *real* reason he wanted to go to Patrick's wasn't because he'd disappoint Tess and Roger if he didn't go. It was because Patrick was rich. Patrick had *everything*, and Ben wanted to see his new birthday presents and play in his big yard. It would be exciting to go to Patrick's house.

Sam was a nice guy, but it wouldn't be exciting to go to his house. After all, he lived in a tiny house and had to share a room with three brothers.

Ben knew he would go to Patrick's house after school. He knew it was wrong, but he wanted to go there so badly, he would do it anyway.

"Uh, Sam," Ben said, "I forgot to tell you something."

"What?" Sam said.

"I can't come over today," Ben said. "I have to go to the dentist. My mom reminded me this morning. I'm sorry."

Sam's face fell, and Ben felt terrible. Sam looked so disappointed.

"Oh," Sam said. "Okay."

"How about tomorrow?" Ben said. "I could come tomorrow."

"I have to take care of my little sister," Sam said. "My mom's not going to be home for a couple of hours after school, and I promised her I'd baby-sit."

"Oh," Ben said, "I'm sorry."

"That's okay," Sam said. "Maybe next week or something."

"Sure!" Ben said. "Let's get together then."

The next kid was up at bat and kicked the ball hard. Ben took off and ran all the way to home. His team cheered for him and clapped him on the back, but he didn't feel very happy. He was thinking about letting Sam down.

But it was still going to be fun at Patrick's house. Ben decided to think about that instead.

After school, Ben, Tess, and Roger walked home with Patrick.

"I wish we'd brought our swimming suits," Tess said, looking wistfully at the sparkling blue water in Patrick's pool.

"Me too," Ben said.

"Me three," Roger said. He looked around the patio and stared up at the huge house. "This sure is a great place, Patrick."

"Thanks," Patrick said. "Come up to my room. I want to show you my new birthday stuff."

"Great!" the three kids said.

They trooped inside and up to the third floor. Patrick led them to his room, but Ben, Tess, and Roger stopped in the doorway.

"This is *your* room, Patrick?" Tess asked. "It's as big as my family's living room!"

"Come on in," Patrick said.

The kids walked into the room. Tess was right. Patrick's bedroom was huge and took up a third of the top floor. At one end was his huge bed. Then there was a large oak dresser with a big-screen TV sitting next to it, facing his bed. A desk with a computer and printer took up part of one long wall.

Over the desk was a bulletin board

crammed full of colorful picture postcards. Ben had never seen so many postcards. There must have been two hundred of them!

"Wow!" Ben said. "Where did all of these cards come from?"

"From my mom and dad," Patrick said. "Whenever they have to travel on business, they send me postcards."

"Boy, they must travel a lot!" Tess said.

Patrick's smile faded a little. Then he brightened again. "Hey, look what my dad gave me for my birthday!" he said.

He raced to a closet door and pulled it open.

"Zowie!" Tess whispered because she'd never before seen a closet that big. The entire third-grade class could fit inside!

Patrick pulled out a tall instrument on wheels and pulled it over in front of the window.

"Your own telescope!" Ben squealed. "Awesome!"

"It's really, really powerful," Patrick said.

Roger walked over to Patrick and put his hand gently on the telescope. "This is beautiful," he said in a voice full of awe. "Just beautiful."

"Have you looked at the stars?" Ben asked.

"Well, not yet," Patrick said. "But as soon as my dad gets home, he said he'd help me find all the stars and constellations."

"When does he get home?" Ben asked.

"The 25th," Patrick said.

"*Today's* the 25th!" Ben said.

"No, next month," Patrick said.

"How long has he been gone?" Tess asked.

"About a week," Patrick said. "Mom and Dad both went for their business."

"Gee, that's a long time," Tess said.

Patrick sat down on the edge of the bed. "Yeah," was all he said, but Ben could see the disappointment in Patrick's eyes. He was missing his mom and dad.

"Do they always travel a lot?" Ben asked.

"Yeah," Patrick said. "They're gone every month."

"Don't ya miss them?" Tess asked. Ben thought Tess shouldn't have asked Patrick that question, and he scowled at her.

"Yeah, I miss them," Patrick said. He stared at the floor.

No one spoke for a moment. The mood had changed in the room.

"But Hildy takes care of you," Ben said, trying to make Patrick feel better. "She's almost like family, isn't she?"

"Well, sort of," Patrick said. "But she has her own family. She's always talking about them, her nieces and nephews and brothers and sisters." He sighed. "I wish I had brothers and sisters."

"I don't have brothers and sisters," Roger said, "and I don't miss having them."

"Do your mom and dad travel a lot?" Patrick asked him.

"No," Roger admitted. "Just when we take our summer vacation together."

Patrick nodded. "At least when they go somewhere, you get to go too."

"Listen, Patrick," Tess said, "having brothers and sisters isn't all that great. I have a sister who's 15. We have to share a room, and she drives me crazy."

"Yeah," Patrick said. He smiled a little but didn't say anything more.

The kids looked at his telescope, and then Patrick showed them his big remote-control airplane, which they flew over the huge back lawn.

Ben watched Patrick while they played and thought about his rich friend. Maybe Patrick wasn't quite as lucky as he'd thought.

It would be great to have that big room and all those toys and expensive things to play with. But it sure wouldn't be as much fun to have all that stuff if your parents didn't have time to spend with you.

Ben imagined what it would be like not to have his mom and dad with him at home. They wouldn't be able to play their weekly game of Monopoly together or toss the ball around the backyard. Their trips to the park pool on family swim nights wouldn't happen. And what if, like Patrick, he had to spend his birthday with servants instead of with his parents?

That made him feel lonely.

Ben still wanted to be rich, but only if everything else in his life remained exactly the same.

Supper with Sam

Ben played at Patrick's house the next afternoon and the next. They swam in the pool, rode Patrick's horse, and flew the new remote-control airplane.

Ben had a wonderful time.

"Let's play at *your* house on Saturday," Patrick said to Ben when they had successfully landed the plane for the last time one afternoon.

Ben stared at Patrick, shocked. "Why would you want to do *that?*" he said.

"I've never been to your house," Patrick said.

Ben gulped. He thought of his small, one-story house and his little bedroom.

"But I don't have—well, I mean, there

isn't as much to do at my house," Ben said. "We don't have a pool or anything."

"That's okay," Patrick said, shrugging. "We could play in your room."

Ben caught his breath. Patrick must not have any idea how small Ben's room was! There was hardly room enough for Ben to play there alone, and he didn't want Patrick to see how small it was. He was sure that Patrick would feel sorry for him the way Ben felt sorry for Sam Flagg.

Then he had an idea. "I know," Ben said. "Let's go to the park on Saturday. I'll meet you by the swings, and I'll bring my football."

"Okay," Patrick said. "That'll be fun."

Ben sighed with relief. Now Patrick wouldn't have to see his room. Ben didn't have even a fourth as much stuff to play with as Patrick!

So on Saturday afternoon, Ben took his football and met Patrick at the park by the swings. They passed the ball back and forth.

Ben liked to play football. He liked running and diving to catch the ball, feeling the warm sun on his face and the breeze in his hair. He was glad to see how much farther he could throw the ball than last year.

Patrick was a pretty good football player too, Ben thought. They were evenly matched.

"Hi, Ben! Hi, Patrick!" a voice called out from the sidewalk next to the park.

Ben turned and saw Sam Flagg. With him was a boy about four.

"Hey, Sam!" Ben called out. "Come on over and play football with us."

"Can't," Sam said. "I'm watching my brother so my mom can get some work done." He grinned. "You guys look hot. Want to come over for awhile? Mom made some lemonade."

"Sure," Patrick said. "Lemonade sounds great."

"Yeah," Ben said. He was glad Patrick wanted to go over to Sam's house. Everybody knew Sam was poor, but Patrick didn't seem to mind at all.

If Patrick didn't mind being at Sam's house, Ben thought, maybe he wouldn't mind his house either.

The boys walked home with Sam and clomped up the sagging porch steps to the front door. A girl about 10 was curled up in the porch swing reading a book.

"Hi, Beck," Sam said. He turned to the boys. "This is my sister, Becky. All she does is read."

Becky didn't even look up from the page she was reading. She held up her hand in a wave and mumbled, "I'm at the best part."

Sam rolled his eyes and pulled open the screen door. Good smells came from the kitchen, where a clanking of dishes could be heard.

Sam led the boys into the kitchen. "Mom, could we have some lemonade?"

Mrs. Flagg looked up from a roaster she'd just pulled out of the oven. "Hi, boys," she said, smiling. "Help yourselves."

Sam introduced the boys to his mother as he filled three glasses with cold lemonade.

"I'm glad to meet you, boys," Mrs. Flagg said. "I've heard so many nice things about both of you, Ben and Patrick."

Once again, Ben felt guilty about not playing with Sam the other day. Sam really was a nice kid, just as nice as Patrick. He shouldn't have lied to Sam about having to go to the dentist.

Mrs. Flagg took the cover off the roaster and a cloud of steam billowed up to the ceiling. A turkey, brown and plump, hissed in juices inside the pan. She filled a baster with the liquid at the bottom of the pan and squirted it over the bird.

"Mmmm, that smells good!" Sam said.

"Glad to hear it," said Mrs. Flagg. "We'll be eating as soon as your dad gets home from running errands. He just called and is on his way."

"Could Ben and Patrick stay for dinner?" asked Sam.

Mrs. Flagg smiled. "Well, tonight we *do* have plenty of food," she said. "This is a big turkey! The A & P had a special sale yesterday, so I thought we'd sample Thanksgiving a little early this year."

Sam whirled around to Ben and Patrick. "Want to stay?"

Ben's mouth was watering. "Yeah!" he said. "I just have to call my mom."

"I'll call Hildy," Patrick said, "but I'm sure it'll be okay."

The boys called and got permission to stay.

An older boy walked into the kitchen. "When're we eating, Mom?" he said.

"Soon," she said. "You're just in time to help me, Josh. Would you drain those potatoes, please, so I can mash them? Oh, Sam, stand here and stir the gravy, will you? I don't want it to get lumpy. But first call Pete to put milk in the glasses. Ben and Patrick, will you help Ann set the table? Ann!" she called out. "Come and set the table! Two extra places tonight."

Ann walked in from the living room. Ben remembered seeing her in Roger's class at school. Ann was as blond as Sam was dark, and he would never have guessed they were related. Ann handed Ben the plates and Patrick the knives, forks, and spoons.

Everybody got to work, and there was a lot of talking and laughing and bustling back and forth between the kitchen cupboards and the table. It was fun to be put to work with everyone else, Ben thought. It made him feel welcome, almost as if he were part of the family.

Ben set the plates down on the table, then glanced over at Patrick. Very carefully, Patrick laid out the tableware on the long picnic table along the far wall of the kitchen.

"There!" he said to Ann when he had finished. "How does it look?"

Ann grinned. "Excellent," she said, "only the knives go between the plates and the spoons."

"Oh," Patrick said. He set about switching the position of all the knives.

Ben couldn't help smiling. Patrick, who was used to having servants do all the chores at his house, was having *fun* setting the table!

"Ta-DA!" Patrick said when he'd finished. He looked at Ann for approval.

"I couldn't have done it better myself," said Ann. She clapped Patrick on the shoulder, then she disappeared into the kitchen.

Patrick looked over at Ben and grinned. "Thanksgiving dinner," he said. "This is great."

"Yeah," Ben said.

As soon as Sam's father arrived, everyone sat down at the picnic table.

"Ben, Patrick," said Mrs. Flagg, "would you like to join us in the blessing? We hold hands."

Ben and Patrick joined hands with the Flagg family, creating a huge circle of clasped hands around the table.

"It's your turn, Sam," said Mr. Flagg.

"Oh, right," Sam said. "Okay."

They all bowed their heads.

"Father," Sam said, "we thank You for this beautiful turkey that Mom got on sale yesterday. Thank You for giving us everything we need, like food, clothes, our house, our health, and—and good friends like Ben and Patrick to share all that stuff with. Amen."

"Amen," echoed nine voices around the table.

Ben glanced at Patrick across the table. Patrick's face was filled with awe. He seemed to be enjoying himself, sitting at dinner with this big family.

"Very nice blessing, Sam," said Mr. Flagg.

"Yes, it was," said Mrs. Flagg. "We don't have turkey and all the trimmings more than a few times a year, but we should celebrate Thanksgiving every day. We have so much to be thankful for."

"Emma," said Mr. Flagg. "I don't believe I've ever seen a finer looking turkey."

He picked up a fork and a large carving knife and began cutting slices of turkey for each member of the family. Bowls of mashed potatoes, gravy, hot rolls, green beans, and fruit salad were passed hand to hand down and around the table.

"Dig in!" said Luke, the little brother who had been with Sam at the park.

Everyone ate. The conversation at the table was lively and fun. When the dinner was almost over, Luke piped up, "Can I start The Telling?"

"Sure," said Mr. Flagg.

"The Telling?" asked Patrick. "What's that?"

"At the end of every meal," said Sam, "we go around the table and tell what we did today."

Mr. Flagg smiled. "In a family as big as this one, you have to do that to keep track of what everybody's up to."

"So can I start?" asked Luke.

"You have our undivided attention," said Mrs. Flagg.

"Well," said Luke, "this morning, Sam

and I went down to Morgan Creek and threw rocks into the water. Then we went over to Hendersons and looked at their kittens. They have *two batches* of 'em!"

"How many kittens in the two batches?" asked Becky.

"Um, three and four," Luke said. He stopped and counted silently on his fingers. He held up seven fingers. "Seven. Seven kittens."

"Luke, your counting is getting better and better," said Mrs. Flagg.

"Yeah, then we walked home and had lunch," said Luke.

"What about this afternoon?" asked Mr. Flagg.

"Sam and I watched the big hot-air balloons take off from the vacant lot," said Luke. "They went really high!"

"I would've liked to see that," said Mr. Flagg.

And that's the way it went. Everybody had a turn in The Telling, including Ben and Patrick. Every person was given polite attention by the nine others around the table, who asked questions to find out more.

Ben looked around the table and listened

to each person tell what had happened during the day. Every face at the table looked happy and interested in one another.

After dinner the family moved into the living room. Ben looked around the room. There was no television.

Sam's three brothers and two sisters picked up books or pulled out board games from the cupboard and settled down for a quiet evening together.

"Where's your TV?" Ben asked Sam.

"We don't have one now," he said. "It broke last year, and we didn't have the money to get it fixed. After that, I guess we forgot about it."

Patrick's mouth popped open. "You *forgot?*"

Sam laughed. "Yeah, I like to read more now than I used to, and Josh's grades are *way* better than they were at the beginning of last year." He shrugged. "Sometimes I miss the TV, but most of the time I don't even think about it."

Ben and Patrick stayed for a game of Monopoly with Sam, Pete, and Ann, and then it was time to go home.

Ben and Patrick walked down the front walk and turned to head home on Clover Road.

"Man," Patrick said, shuffling along, "Sam is so lucky."

"Yeah," Ben said.

And that's when it hit him.

Sam Flagg—the poorest kid in his class, the kid who had to wear clothes that didn't fit, who had to share a bedroom with three other brothers, who didn't even have a TV—Sam Flagg was *lucky*.

No, Ben thought, that wasn't quite right. Sam Flagg was *blessed*. He was blessed with the riches Mrs. Pilkington had talked about. He had a great family who loved one other and spent time together.

Ben glanced over at Patrick and was shocked to realize that he felt a little sorry for his friend. Patrick didn't see much of his mom and dad. He spent his birthday with servants.

Ben realized that even though he didn't have a big family like Sam, he had also received wonderful blessings from God. His mother and father loved him and made him feel safe and important. And Grady was a great little brother.

And that, Ben thought, was even better than money.

5

A New Member
of the Club

"It is our privilege," said Roger in a low, serious voice, "to make you, Mrs. Miriam Pilkington, an honorary member of The Tree House Kids."

Mrs. Pilkington, sitting crossed-legged on the tree house floor with Roger, Ben, and Tess, bent down a little, and Roger slipped a necklace made of a wide red ribbon over her head.

From the ribbon dangled a round piece of flat cardboard that said *The Tree House Kids— Honorary Member* painted in bright red letters.

"Congratulations," said Roger.

Tess and Ben applauded politely.

"Thank you!" said Mrs. P. "That was a lovely ceremony. I'm sure Mr. Pilkington would be happy to know that the tree house he built for our son is being used by such nice young—"

Roger leaned over and tugged on Mrs. P.'s sleeve. "The ceremony isn't over yet, Mrs. P.," he whispered.

"Oh," Mrs. P. said, putting her hand over her mouth to try and hide her smile. "Oh, I am sorry!"

"Ben will now sing The Tree House Kids theme song, which he wrote for this special occasion," Roger said in his serious voice again.

"Yeah," interrupted Tess, "but we've been bugging him for a month to do it!"

"Shh!" said Roger. He looked at Ben. "Go ahead, Ben."

Ben nodded, then stood. He cleared his throat, and to the tune of "America, the Beautiful," he sang:

The Tree House Kids, The Tree House Kids,
To you we are true blue!
We get along, we sing this song,
Up here there's such a view!

Whenever times are hard or bad,
Our helping hands we lend.
Here is a clue, we stick like glue,
We always have a friend!

Roger, Tess, and Mrs. Pilkington clapped.

"*Now* it's over," said Roger to Mrs. P. He uncovered a plate of brownies and pulled a thermos and paper cups out of a paper bag. "Time for the refreshments."

"Thank you, kids," said Mrs. P. "I'm very honored to be a member of your club. And Ben, that was a very nice theme song."

Ben grinned. "Thanks," he said. "I worked on it for an hour last night!"

"Write it down, Ben, and give us copies so we can learn it," said Tess. "We should sing it at all our meetings."

"Good idea," said Roger.

"Okay," said Ben.

"Have a brownie," Roger said to Mrs. P., holding the plate out to her. "I made them myself."

"Good for you, Roger," said Mrs. P. "I'd love one."

They all helped themselves.

"Mrs. P.," said Ben, "remember what you said about us being rich?"

"Yes," said Mrs. P., chewing a bite of brownie. "Oh, Roger, this is delicious."

"Thanks," Roger said, grinning.

"Well," said Ben, "when you said that, I didn't really think you were right. I mean, I knew I had a great family and everything, but I still wanted money. And lots of stuff, like Patrick."

"You sure played with him a lot this week," said Tess.

"Yeah," said Ben. "But Patrick and I went over to Sam Flagg's house yesterday. I always thought how poor he was, and I felt sorry for him. But he's *really* not poor at all!"

"You mean, Sam's family has money?" said Tess. "How could they? Sam always wears old, old clothes!"

"No," said Ben, "they don't have much money. But Sam has this big family, and they all sit around a picnic table in the kitchen to eat."

Ben explained how every member of the family pitches in to work on supper. He told them about The Telling after each meal, and how they all read and played games together because they didn't have a TV.

"I'd hate it if we didn't have a TV," said Tess.

"But they have so much fun!" said Ben. "Even Patrick thought Sam was lucky."

"*Really?*" said Tess. "Well, I guess Patrick did seem kind of lonely when we were over at his house."

"A bulletin board full of postcards sure isn't as good as having a mom and dad at home," said Roger.

"Yeah," Ben said. "So I've been thinking. I don't need a lot more money. I mean, I'd like it if my family could go to Great Adventures more often, but I guess I really *am* rich, just like you said, Mrs. P."

Mrs. Pilkington smiled. "You know something, Ben?" she said. "You're a very mature young man."

Ben's cheeks tinted pink. "Really?" he said.

"Really," said Mrs. Pilkington. "And I think you're absolutely right about your being rich." She looked around the circle of kids. "You're all rich."

"I wouldn't *mind* having a million dollars,

though," Tess said around a mouthful of brownie.

Mrs. Pilkington laughed.

Ben grinned. "I wouldn't either. But I don't want to be the richest kid in the world anymore."

"You don't?" said Tess.

"Nope," said Ben. "I think I already *am* the richest kid in the world. Me and Sam Flagg."

"And me," said Tess.

"And me," said Roger.

"You bet," said Mrs. Pilkington. "And I'm richer for having you three as my friends."

"We four are really lucky—I mean, really blessed, aren't we?" said Ben.

"We are, indeed," said Mrs. P. "We are, indeed."